# Secret World

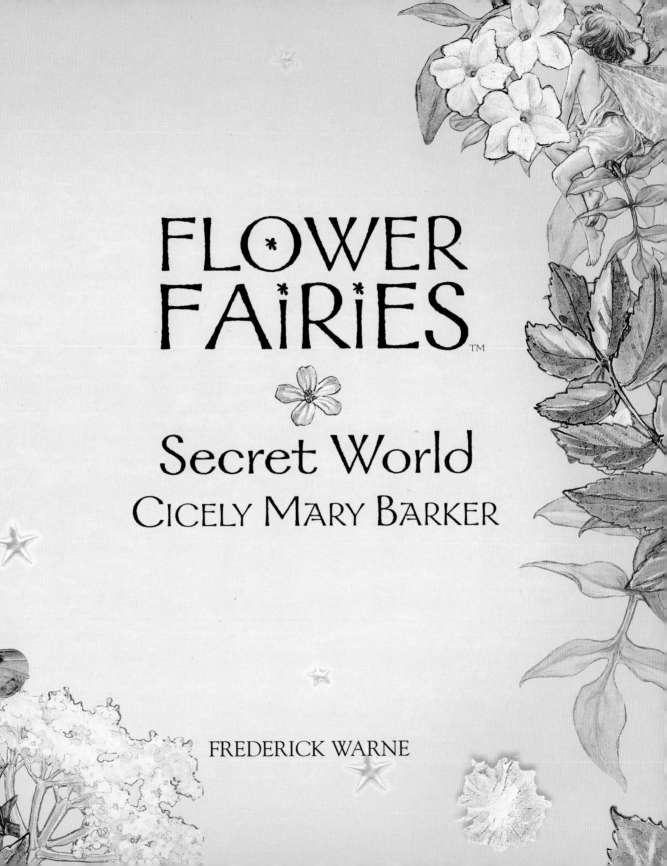

# FLOWER FAIRIES ™

## Secret World

### CICELY MARY BARKER

FREDERICK WARNE

Do you believe in fairies? This book is all about the secret world of the Flower Fairies. It is rare to see a Flower Fairy. Like most fairies they are extremely shy of big people, and you will only see them if you believe in them.

I believe in fairies.

Signed.................................................................

Can you see Foxglove hiding in his flowers?

Burdock tiptoes quietly

Elderberry looks down from above

Blackthorn climbs up her spiky branches

Where are the fairies?
Where can we find them?
We've seen the fairy-rings
They leave behind them!

Is it a secret
No one is telling?
Why, in your garden
Surely they're dwelling!

No need for journeying,
Seeking afar:
Where there are flowers,
There fairies are!

Red Campion peeps out from
the woodland's edge

Whenever a seed sprouts, a Flower Fairy baby boy or girl is born. The little baby sleeps hidden under its leaves, and as the plant grows taller, its fairy grows up too.

There is probably a Flower Fairy not very far away from you at this very moment, looking after a tree or flower. Flower Fairies sweep away dead leaves, and polish up new ones. They keep their flower petals shaped, clean and tidy. And every Flower Fairy helps with the important job of sowing seeds, and watering the new seedlings.

Snip,snip,snip,

go busy Pink

Black Medick looks after the seed heads

Dainty Shirley Poppy helps to sow seeds

...scissors

Herb Twopence talks to his seedling

What are Flower Fairies like? They worry about the weather, and insects eating their plant's leaves, as well as humans picking their plants and dropping rubbish. But Flower Fairies also love music and dancing, and having fun. They do all they can to help each other look after the countryside, and they are the nicest and kindest of all the fairies.

Periwinkle's flowers are a beautiful blue

Primrose is one of the first flowers of spring

Harebell's blossoms are like dainty bells

Daisy flowers make the prettiest garlands

All Flower Fairies are born with tiny wings and pointy ears

All fairies are 2-4 inches tall, that's 6-10 fairy feet!

By the time they are fully grown, Flower Fairies have wings as strong and colourful as butterfly wings

Dogwood's leaves are bronze and crimson

Box Tree likes to live in gardens

Winter Aconite doesn't mind the cold

Forget-me-not lies on a bed of leaves

Ribwort Plantain whistles a tune for his snail

The Fuchsia Fairy

The Gaillardia Fairy

Gaillardia wears shorts and boots made from his leaves

Fuchsia's dress looks exactly like her bell-shaped flowers

The White Bindweed Fairy

The Cornflower Fairy

White Bindweed's bonnet is made from her leaves

Cornflower wears a crown of blue flower

The Fumitory Fairy

The Marigold Fairy

The Sloe Fairy

Fumitory's skirts are the colours of her plant

Look at Marigold's necklace of golden petals

Sloe has spots on her dress just like her berries

Flower Fairies have very special clothes. Everyone wears an outfit which is made from the leaves and petals of their own plant or flower, and this makes it easy for them to hide among the leaves and flowers.

Bugle's bonnet is a bugle blossom

Flower Fairy boys and girls are proud of their clever disguises.

Seed pods, petals, buds and leaves become sweet bonnets, shoes and bags, and buttons are made from dried seeds.

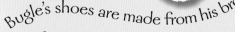

Bugle's shoes are made from his bronzy leaves

Wayfaring Tree's leaves are cleverly stitched together to make her hat

Look at Wayfaring Tree's sandals, they match her handbag!

If a Flower Fairy's dress needs patching, she will pick a petal or leaf from her plant and take it to Tansy, the fairy who mends clothes. Tansy uses a needle from a pine tree and her thread is made from dried grass.

Were ever such button-like flowers seen—

Yellow, for elfin coats of green?

Three in a row — I stitch them so!

Lavender's blue, lavender's green
She'll scent the clothes, put away clean—
Clean from the wash, hanky and sheet;
Lavender's spikes, make them all sweet!

Lavender washes all the
Flower Fairies' clothes.
She uses soap made with her
own sweet-smelling flowers.
On a windy day, Lavender
hangs the clothes up to dry,
pegged out on bushes, or on
washing lines strung up
between tufts of grass.

Little Blue-tit keeps Winter Jasmine company

Flower Fairies let butterflies and bees drink nectar from their flowers. During the coldest winters, fairies huddle together with the mice in their burrows and birds in their nests to keep warm, so they are happy to share their seeds and nuts with these friendly creatures.

Snapdragon is pleased to see Bumble Bee collecting pollen

Red Clover greets her own Bee friend

Hazel-nut gathers her ripe nuts

Flower Fairies eat nuts and berries. With honey from the bees, and fruit from their trees, they make fragrant wines, sweet jams, and delicious fairy jellies.

Mallow's seeds make the finest fairy cheeses

Crab-apple catches her apples to make scrumptious jelly

Apple Blossom is the most bossy, and sits on her branch telling the babies what to do

Just like humans, Flower Fairies need to be cared for when they are young. The babies crawl and clamber around their plants, falling off and getting into mischief. So, the older Flower Fairies look after the little ones.

Guelder Rose shows her little sister how to look after their flowers

Sweet Pea is the gentlest, and likes to dress the babies up in pretty clothes

Silver Birch and Sycamore
teach the babies how to swing
around their plants safely

Every single older Flower Fairy has the job of
teaching the young ones how to care for their plant.
But a lot of the time, Flower Fairy babies just play!

Pansy teaches dance

Flower Fairy homes are all around you, but they are cleverly hidden. A human would not recognise a Flower Fairy home, we would just see a few bent blades of grass or a pile of twigs and leaves.

Garden Flower Fairies are the most sociable. A lot of them live in parks or town gardens, so of course they are used to traffic noise and human voices, and not as easily frightened. Garden fairies enjoy company. They are confident, friendly and talkative!

Wallflower loves to sit high up on the wall

Tulip is always welcome in the garden

Lily-of-the-valley rings her snowy white bells

Grape Hyacinth chats to the others

Double Daisy greets the sun with a smile

Totter-grass likes to dance alone in the breeze

Buttercup's golden blossoms flourish all summer long

Poppy stands tall and splendid

Delicate and pretty, wild fairies live peacefully alongside country lanes and footpaths. They play together, and sometimes you can hear them calling to each other (their voices sound like bird song).

Little White Clover is gentle and sweet

Rush-grass and Cotton-grass guide travellers across the moors

The wind-swept fields and meadows are home to the nomadic grass fairies. They have no particular home, and at night they just crawl under a leaf to sleep.

Old-man's-beard sleeps on his bed of fluffy seeds

Wild Cherry Blossom sits among her clouds of white blossoms

Treetop fairies are the most daring and athletic of all Flower Faires. The blossom fairies have no fear of heights. They are happiest swinging from branch to branch high up in their trees. They are the fairy acrobats!

Pear Blossom sings to the birds

Lilac blossoms have the sweetest scent of all

The watery fairies play near their homes on the banks of rivers and streams. Sometimes you can hear their silvery voices, which sound a bit like running water.

Willow dips her leaves in the cool water

Naughty Horse Chestnut lives high in the trees

Beechnut is the naughtiest of all

The youngest
nut fairies are the
naughtiest, playing noisy
games of chase in their
branches. If you are walking under
a beech tree on a blustery day, it is
not the wind that sends the
beechnuts raining down
onto your head!

Alder loves to play by the river

Look up, look up, at any tree!
There is so much for eyes to see:
And, if you're quick enough, maybe
A laughing fairy in the tree!

Iris plays at the water's edge

Canterbury bells play a merry tune

Flower Fairies love music and dance.
The King and the Queen of the Flower
Fairies love to have parties in their fairy court,
and everyone joins in. Flower Fairies have lots
to celebrate. Four times a year, they throw a big
ball to usher in the start of spring, summer,
autumn and winter.

Almond Blossom dances for the court

Rose-bay Willow-herb sways to the music

Columbine is the star fairy ballerina

Honeysuckle's trumpet sounds from way up high

When the fairies hear Canterbury Bell's flowers ringing, they know a party is about to start. The Flower Fairies begin to gather, coming from far and wide. The singing and dancing goes on late into the night. The next day there are a lot of sleepy Flower Fairies dozing under their plants!

Queen of the Meadow watches the dancing

Kingcup is King of the fairies

Ragged Robin pipes a merry tune

Ground Ivy stays up late to peep at the party

To shop, and school, to work and play,
The busy people pass all day;
They hurry, hurry, to and fro,
And hardly notice as they go
The wayside flowers, known so well,
Whose names so few of them can tell.
They never think of fairy-folk
Who may be hiding for a joke!

Cherry's fruit is a treat for the birds

Candytuft watches over the others

Geranium grows happily in any garden

Narcissus announces the spring

Heliotrope smells her sweet blossoms

Rose's scent lingers in the air

Acorn's seeds grow into the noble oak tree

O, if these people understood
What's to be found by field and wood;
What fairy secrets are made plain
By any footpath, road, or lane—
They'd go with open eyes and look,
(As you will, when you've read this book)
And then at least they'd learn to see
How pretty common things can be!

Yew sits dreaming in his branches

Ash's seeds hang
like bunches of keys

Only the Christmas Tree Fairy
has a wand

Blackberry's berries grow in shiny clusters

Holly's leaves stay green in winter

FREDERICK WARNE

Published by the Penguin Group
Penguin Books Ltd, 80 Strand, London WC2R 0RL, England
Penguin Young Readers Group, 375 Hudson Street, New York, New York 10014, USA
Penguin Books Australia Ltd, 250 Camberwell Road, Camberwell, Victoria 3124, Australia
Penguin Books Canada Ltd, 10 Alcorn Avenue, Toronto, Ontario, Canada M4V 3B2
Penguin Books India (P) Ltd, 11 Community Centre,
Panchsheel Park, New Delhi 110 017, India
Penguin Books (NZ) Ltd, Cnr Airborne and Rosedale Roads, Albany, Auckland 1310, New Zealand
Penguin Books (South Africa) (Pty) Ltd, P O Box 9, Parklands 2121, South Africa

Penguin Books Ltd, Registered Offices: 80 Strand, London WC2R 0RL, England

**Web site at: www.flowerfairies.com**

First published by Frederick Warne 2002
1 3 5 7 9 10 8 6 4 2

ISBN 0 7232 5685 3

Printed and bound in China